This LADYBIRD TALE
belongs to

....

The Little
Red Hen

Retold by Vera Southgate M.A., B.COM
with illustrations by Mélanie Florian

LADYBIRD 🐞 TALES

ONCE UPON A TIME there was a little red hen who lived in a farmyard.

One day the little red hen found some grains of wheat.

She took them to the other animals in the farmyard.

"Who will help me to plant
these grains of wheat?" asked
the little red hen.

"Not I," said the cat.

"Not I," said the rat.

"Not I," said the pig.

"Then I shall plant the grains myself," said the little red hen.

So she did.

Every day the little red hen went to the field to watch the grains of wheat growing.

They grew tall and strong.

One day, the little red hen saw that the wheat was ready to be cut.

"Now the wheat can be made into flour," said the little red hen to herself, as she set off for the farmyard.

"Who will help me to take the wheat to the mill, to be ground into flour?" asked the little red hen.

"Not I," said the cat.

"Not I," said the rat.

"Not I," said the pig.

"Then I shall take the wheat to the mill myself," said the little red hen.

So she did.

The little red hen took the wheat to the mill and the miller ground it into flour.

When the wheat had been ground
into flour, the little red hen
took it to the other animals
in the farmyard.

"Who will help me to take this flour to the baker to be made into bread?" asked the little red hen.

"Not I," said the cat.

"Not I," said the rat.

"Not I," said the pig.

"Then I shall take the flour to the baker myself," said the little red hen.

So she did.

The little red hen took the flour
to the baker and the baker made
it into bread.

When the bread was baked,
the little red hen took it to the
other animals in the farmyard.

"The bread is now ready to
be eaten," said the little red hen.
"Who will help me to eat
the bread?"

"I will," said the cat.

"I will," said the rat.

"I will," said the pig.

"No, you will not," said the little red hen. "I shall eat it myself."

So she did.

A History of
The Little Red Hen

The Little Red Hen is an old folk tale. Some sources say it originates from England, while others suggest it is from Russia. Regardless of the tale's history, it has continued to be passed down over the centuries, and it remains as popular today as ever.

The tale has changed little over the years. Its simple narrative teaches that if you work hard, you will be rewarded. The story depicts a hard-working hen who plants the grain, tends to the plants and cuts the wheat all by herself. It is she, alone, who takes the wheat to be ground into flour and baked to make a loaf of bread, without the help of her farmyard friends.

As such, after all her hard work, the little red hen is rightly the only animal in the farmyard to enjoy the bread.

Ladybird's 1966 edition, retold by Vera Southgate, has ensured the tale continues to reach a new generation of readers.

Collect more fantastic

LADYBIRD 🐞 TALES

Little Red Riding Hood

9781409311126

Goldilocks and the Three Bears

9781409311119

Cinderella

9781409311072

Jack and the Beanstalk

9781409311102

The Gingerbread Man

9781409311096

The Three Little Pigs

9781409311089

The Three Billy Goats Gruff

9781409311065

Hansel and Gretel

9781409311133

Puss in Boots

9781409311225

Rapunzel

9781409311195

Rumpelstiltskin

9781409311164

The Elves and the Shoemaker

9781409311188

Snow White
and the
Seven Dwarfs

9781409311171

The Enormous
Turnip

9781409311218

The Magic
Porridge Pot

9781409311201

Sleeping
Beauty

9781409311157

The Princess
and the Frog

9780718192556

Dick
Whittington

9780718192532

The Big
Pancake

9780718192549

Beauty
and the Beast

9780718192587

The Little
Red Hen

9780718192525

The Ugly
Duckling

9780718193133

The Princess
and the Pea

9780718192570

Chicken
Licken

9780718192563

Endpapers taken from series 606d,
first published in 1964

A catalogue record for this book is available from the British Library

Published by Ladybird Books Ltd
80 Strand London WC2R 0RL
A Penguin Company

002

ISBN: 978-0-71819-252-5

Printed in China